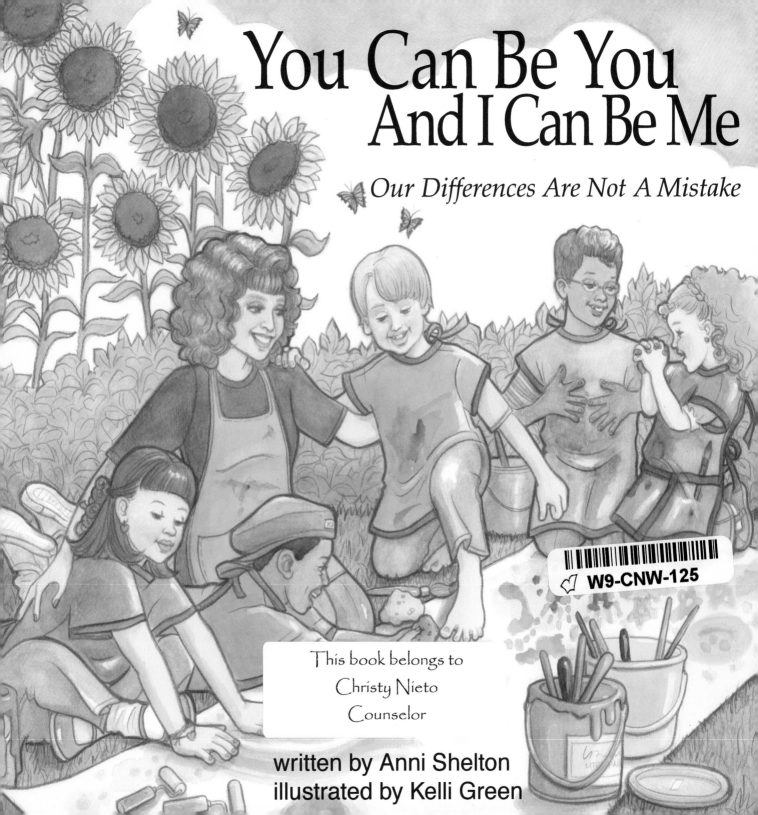

You Can Be You
And I Can Be Me

Our Differences Are Not A Mistake

This book belongs to
Christy Nieto
Counselor

W9-CNW-125

written by Anni Shelton
illustrated by Kelli Green

First published by Dog Ear Publishing
4010 W. 86th Street, Ste H
Indianapolis, IN 46268
www.dogearpublishing.net

ISBN: 1-59858-109-0
Library of Congress Control Number: 2005938658

This book is printed on acid-free paper.
This book is a work of Fiction. Places, events, and situations in this book are purely Fictional
and any resemblance to actual persons, living or dead, is coincidental.

Printed in the United States of America

Dedicated to my Husband, Children and
Grandchildren... my treasures.

And to my Dad...
who says I do everything "write".

You were meant to have hair
that was straight,
but mine was meant to be curly.

You were not meant to be me, and I was not meant to be you,
'Cause no one else can be like me,
and only you can be you!

You were meant to like kisses,
but I was meant to like hugs.

I have always liked orange juice,
but you have always liked milk.

You were made to run and play,
but I was made to think.

You were meant to be you, and I was meant to be me.
That's how God made us. It's how we're supposed to be!

I was meant to like flowers,
but you were meant to like bugs.

You are supposed to be serious,
but I was meant to be squirrelly.

Your favorite color was meant to be purple,
but mine was meant to be pink.

I like the feeling of velvet,
but you like the feeling of silk.

You were meant to like jumping,
but my favorite thing is to read.

You were meant to be shy,
but I was created to lead!

You were meant to be you, and I was meant to be me,
'Cause no one else can be like you,
and only I can be me!

I was meant to be squishy, but you were meant to be strong.

You like to draw pretty pictures,
but I like to sing pretty songs.

You were meant to like dogs,
but I find that I prefer cats.

I like to go window shopping,
but you'd rather never do that!

You were meant to like riding your bike,
but I was meant to like swinging.

You like the sound of the ocean's roar,
but I like the sound of birds singing.

You can order a soda,
and I can order iced tea.

You can eat macaroni,
and I can eat broccoli.

I'm not supposed to be you, and you aren't supposed to be me!
God made all of us special, but each of us differently.

So you go ahead and be happy you're you,
and I'll be happy I'm me.
And we'll both be glad for each other
'Cause it's how we're supposed to be!

The End

About the Author

Anni Shelton has always had a way with words. Whether spoken or written, her passion for communication and her delightful transparency has a way of drawing people in. She has been entertaining, encouraging and influencing people with the things she has written for the past thirty years. Anni is a happily married, ordained minister who stays at home to home school her three youngest children, ages 7, 10 and 13 years old. Her oldest daughter lives five doors down with her husband and four children ages 6, 4, 2 and 6 months old.

Anni Shelton can be reached at moregrace1@aol.com.

About the Illustrator

You Can Be You And I Can Be Me," is the first children's book illustration project for [Kelli] who has, until recently worked mainly as a graphic art designer for small businesses and ministries.

Ms. Green, who holds an Associate in Arts degree in Art & Design, claims she has discovered her niche in [illustrating early readers] stating, "Helping children to see themselves in the uniquely-beautiful way that God sees them is an honor indescribable."

She resides in South Central Pennsylvania where she continues to do freelance work and minister to inner city children and youth.

Ms. Green can be reached at greenlive8@cs.com

If we could ever fully comprehend how adored we really are, all striving would cease... Anni Shelton

CPSIA information can be obtained
at www.ICGtesting.com
228187LV00001B